I dedicate this book to my Lord and tailor
—D. D.

For my dear friend Virginia
—C. S.

Dom DeLuise

King Bob's New Clothes

illustrated by Christopher Santoro

SIMON & SCHUSTER BOOKS FOR YOUNG READERS

LONG, LONG AGO, in a land far, far away—but much closer than you may think—there lived a king whose priorities were all mixed up.

Priorities are those things in your life that are most precious to you, like being kind to your friends and yourself; eating healthily; getting enough sleep; brushing your teeth; keeping clean; having happy, loving thoughts in your head; and doing things that make you feel good. All those are splendid priorities.

This king's name was "Discombobulated"—a name that took much too much time to say, so everyone called him King Bob. He had some strange ideas like, "Clothes make the man," or "You can lead a horse to water, but if you dress him up real nice, you can take him anywhere." And because he was king, no one ever disagreed—because they were afraid.

The king loved clothes—especially fancy new clothes. He would sometimes change his clothing six times in one day. Oh, how he loved to show them off to everyone! You'd think a king would have something better to do.

Now, there lived on a farm in the mountains just outside town, a Mr. and Mrs. Wright, a good and honest man and his good and honest wife. Folks called them Honest John and Honest Jane.

They had a son, a good boy who was called Junior: Honest John, Jr. His mother and father told him to work hard, to keep love in his heart, and always to tell the truth. Junior worked hard on his chores, sometimes with the help of his horse, Harry.

On Sunday, the Wright family would ride their ox, their mule, and their horse, Harry, and go into town to partake of the festivities, which included waving to the king because every Sunday there was a royal procession.

Every Sunday, come Willy or Nilly, the royal subjects would line the streets and wave and cheer as the king would show off his brand new, fancy clothes. Even the fountain in the center of the square seemed extra bubbly when the king walked by.

The band would play peppy royal music. There were four violins, played by the Smith brothers, and the court jester played four trumpets at once! What a strain on his lips, but he *was* good! Two tubas were played by the Sprat twins; and the tambourine, drums, xylophone, and glockenspiel were played by the Zuza family who were all very talented, especially Grandma Zuza.

The king would prance down the streets under his canopy. The canopy was there just in case of rain or drizzle, you know. The canopy was held up by four men whose height was not exactly the same. What a sight!

Sometimes King Bob wore clothes that were so ostentatious (very, very fancy) that people would snicker and wave, laugh and cheer all at the same time. Many of the royal subjects thought, "How foolish our king is!" But no one said a word, because they were afraid.

One day as winter was settling in, two donkeys clip-clopped their way into town. On the donkeys were two out-of-work tailors, Wear and Tear. Wear and Tear Kannive were possibly two of the most dishonest brothers in the whole world. They took advantage of people wherever and whenever they could. They were what we call con men. They liked to pretend. They'd pretend to be kind. They were not. They'd pretend to be caring. They were not. They were so two-faced, if you looked very quickly, you could actually see the four faces! They did have "the gift of gab," however.

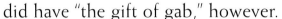

After the townspeople told them all about their king, Wear and Tear went to the castle and asked to see him. They told him they could weave a magical cloth made with gold and silver threads, laced with diamonds, rubies, and emeralds, and that in Europe this magical cloth was all the rage! Very chic, very posh, very in, and that only the pure of heart could see this magic cloth. See, I told you they liked to pretend. Can you imagine anyone believing such a thing?

The king thought, "Gold, silver, diamonds, all the rage, chic, posh, in! That's for me! And since I must be pure of heart, I'm sure to see the cloth."

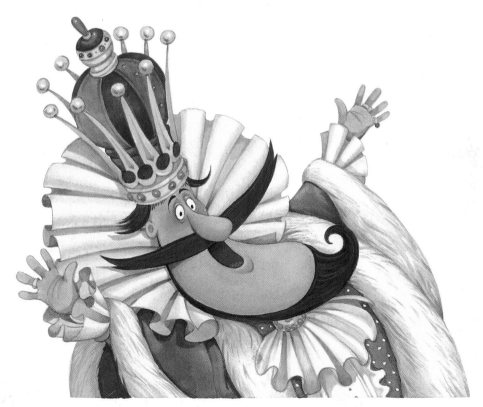

King Bob was so thrilled that he immediately ordered a new royal outfit to be made of the magic cloth. He sent to the treasury for the shiniest gold and silver threads. He sent for diamonds, rubies, and emeralds that sparkled so brightly it would make your eyes go twinkle-twinkle.

The tailors were paid a great deal of money and then set up their loom in a special room where they were to begin their weaving. They took the gold and silver, diamonds, rubies, and emeralds and hid them in their trunk. Then they pretended to begin weaving the magic cloth, reminding everyone that only the "pure of heart" would be able to see it. Since no one wanted to be "impure of heart," they all pretended to see the magic cloth—even the king—because they were all afraid.

The dishonest tailors worked long and hard pretending to make the magic cloth. After many fittings and many high teas with King Bob, the tailors announced that the magical royal robes were ready *and* that it would take at least three people to hold up the train!

"The royal robes are ready!" cried Carlos, the town crier. The very next Sunday, all the people came from every nook and cranny to see the king's new clothes. As a light snow was falling, everyone began lining the streets. Some brought picnic lunches with king crab cakes, chicken à la king, and kings in a blanket. The Wright family was there, of course, because they loved their king. Junior sat high on Harry the horse so he could see above the crowd.

"Look, look! The royal procession is coming!" shouted Big Barbara, the town baker.

"Hear the music! Hooray!"

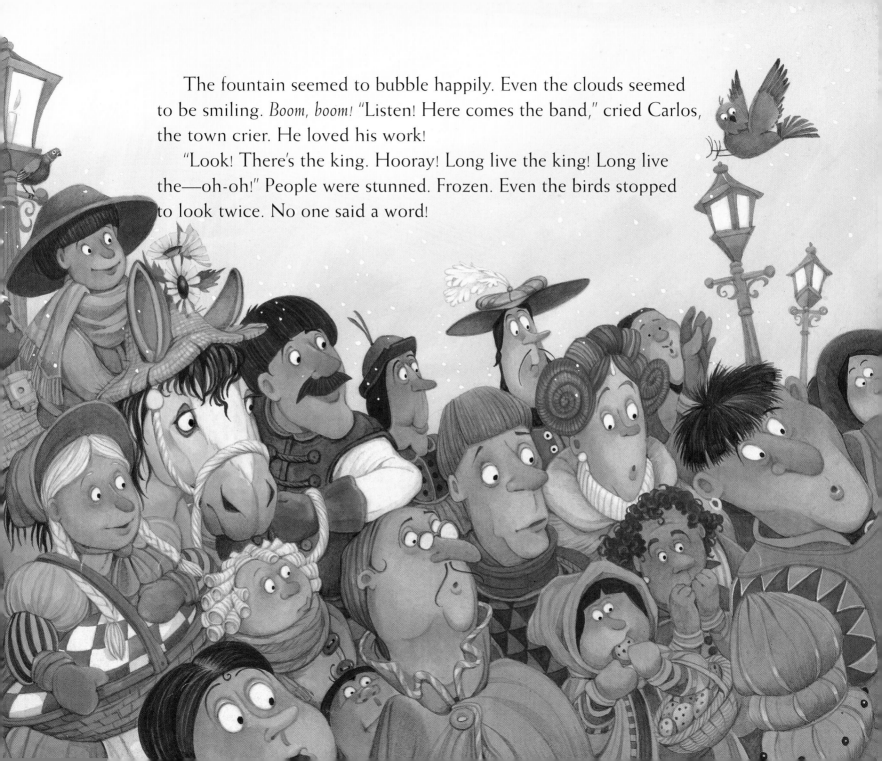

The fountain seemed to bubble happily. Even the clouds seemed to be smiling. *Boom, boom!* "Listen! Here comes the band," cried Carlos, the town crier. He loved his work!

"Look! There's the king. Hooray! Long live the king! Long live the—oh-oh!" People were stunned. Frozen. Even the birds stopped to look twice. No one said a word!

When Honest John, Jr., saw the king, he rubbed his eyes, then he looked again. "The king is naked!" he said. "The king has no clothes on." Everyone gasped! Grandma Zuza fainted. About twelve people said, "Oh, my goodness!" But the little boy just smiled. He had told the truth, and he was *not* afraid.

"What did you say!?" asked the king.

Just then, Walter, the wise man by the side of the road, said, "Out of the mouths of babes, oft' times, comes truth."

"Really?" the king said. "Then bring him here! Bring that boy here!" The king looked straight into the eyes of the little boy. "Do you like my new magical royal robes?"

"What robes?" said Junior.

The king straightened up. "Ah . . . Ah-choo!!" he sneezed, waking up Grandma Zuza.

"God bless you, Your Majesty," said the little boy.

"Oh, yes," repeated all the people. "God bless Your Majesty!"

The king was just about to sneeze again when the boy said, "Here, Your Majesty. Please take this horse blanket. It'll keep you nice and warm." And because he liked the king so much, Junior took off Harry's old straw hat, formed it into a crown, and placed it on the king's cold head.

The king, now covered by Harry the horse's hairy blanket, said, "You mean, it took the innocence of this honest boy to make me understand how foolish I was, pretending to see the magic cloth? Did any of you see the magic cloth?"

Everyone shook their heads. "NO!"

"And you all went along with it?"

The royal subjects said, "Uh-huh!"

"And I was naked all the time?"

"Uh-huh!"

"And you all knew it? You all could see?"

"Uh-huh!"

"I thought I felt a draft!" cried the king.

The king's face grew serious. Slowly he turned toward Wear and Tear, who were just starting to leave with their trunk full of royal goodies! "And what do you two have to say for yourselves?" asked King Bob.

"We . . . we . . . we would like to make a donation of all the gold and silver, diamonds, rubies, and emeralds and give them back . . . to the . . . "

The king interrupted. "You will give them back to the people—*to my loyal subjects!*"

Well, you should have heard the roar of the crowd! What a happy noise! Woof!! Then the king shouted, "You! Wear and Tear!"

Wear and Tear froze in their tracks. "Come here!" said the king. Wear and Tear threw themselves on his mercy. Their timing was perfect because the king had just learned something very important and was feeling very merciful. "Wear and Tear," said the king, "I forgive you. But you will be put to work making warm clothing for all the needy subjects in the kingdom. Ha-ha, a good, honest job at last! Why, if it wasn't for your shenanigans, I never would . . . " This time the king interrupted himself. "Hush! I want to say something to my people."

The court jester blew his bugles, *Ta-ta-ta-tah!* Oh, he was so good! Suddenly everyone was quiet. "Your king realizes that his . . ." The king paused. "That *my* values were all mixed up. So my kingdom was all mixed up. I see now that it is not the clothes on a person's back that are important. What is important is the feeling of love in one's heart. And that will be my highest priority, from this day forth!"

Oh, how the people cheered, and from deep down in their hearts they shouted, "Hooray for our king. Long live the king!"

The king was so happy a tear came to his eye. That happens sometimes. He picked Junior up in his arms. "Long live the king!" whispered Junior. "Long live the king!" The king hugged the boy ever so gently. The crowd cheered with love.

The king smiled.
For the first time in his life,
he smelled like a horse—
but he felt like a king.

Dear Parents:
Young children should never cook by
themselves; however, you might enjoy
helping them prepare some of these
yummy royal dishes.

Chicken à la King

Serves 1 king, 1 queen, 2 out-of-work tailors, or 4–5 town criers

2 tablespoons butter or oil
1 carrot, peeled and thinly sliced
1 small red pepper, diced
6–8 mushrooms, sliced
½ cup fresh or frozen peas
2 cups cooked chicken cut into 1-inch pieces (bite size)
1 can cream of mushroom soup
½ cup milk
½ pound cooked noodles, or 2 cups cooked rice or toast tips

In a nonstick pan, sauté carrots and pepper in butter or oil for about 5 minutes or until tender. Add mushrooms, peas, chicken, cream of mushroom soup, and milk. Stirring gently, heat thoroughly. Serve over noodles, rice, or toast. Garnish with parsley.

So good!

King in a Blanket

Serves 2 hungry kings or 4 royal subjects

1 package chicken or turkey hot dogs
1 container of crescent rolls
mustard

Before cooking, cut one end of each hot dog, making a ½ inch crisscross. Then wrap each hot dog in a crescent roll, leaving the cut end exposed. Cook in a toaster oven or regular oven at 350° for 10 minutes, or until golden brown. Crown is formed when the cut end of the hot dog spreads as it cooks. Use mustard to make eyes, nose, and mouth of the king.

Enjoy!

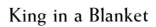
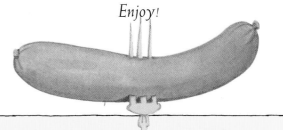

King Crab Cakes

Serves 4 kings or 6 royal subjects

1 pound king crab meat, fresh, frozen, or imitation
3 tablespoons mayonnaise
3 tablespoons mustard
3 eggs
1 small onion, minced
½ green pepper, minced
½ red pepper, minced
1 cup seasoned bread crumbs
1 tablespoon parsley
oil (for cooking)

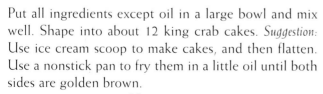

Put all ingredients except oil in a large bowl and mix well. Shape into about 12 king crab cakes. *Suggestion:* Use ice cream scoop to make cakes, and then flatten. Use a nonstick pan to fry them in a little oil until both sides are golden brown.

Yum-yum!

King Crown Cake

Serves 4 crown heads or 4 hungry honest boys

4 pancakes (approximately 6 to 8 inches in diameter)
1 can crushed pineapple
1 container whipped topping
fresh strawberries
candy-coated plain chocolate or nut pieces

Follow directions on your favorite pancake mix. Make 4 pancakes about the same size. Place the first pancake on a platter, then in order spread 2 tablespoons of crushed pineapple and 2 tablespoons of whipped topping between each pancake layer, until all the pancakes are used. Spread remaining whipped topping on top and sides of stack. Place strawberries (rubies) on the top outer rim of the cake. Add the candies as the crown jewels.

HAIL AND EAT HEARTILY.

SIMON & SCHUSTER BOOKS FOR YOUNG READERS
An imprint of Simon & Schuster Children's Publishing Division
1230 Avenue of the Americas
New York, New York 10020

Book design by Anahid Hamparian
The text of this book is set in 15-point Weiss
The illustrations are rendered in watercolor

Manufactured in the United States of America
First Edition

10 9 8 7 6 5 4 3 2

Library of Congress Cataloging-in-Publication Data

DeLuise, Dom.
King Bob's new clothes / by Dom DeLuise ; illustrated by Christopher Santoro.
p.   cm.
Summary: A humorous variation on the fairy tale classic has vain King Bob duped
by two con artists into wearing expensive invisible robes and includes a selection of recipes fit for a king.
[1. Kings, queens, rulers, etc.—Fiction.   2. Pride and vanity—Fiction.
3. Honesty—Fiction]   I. Santoro, Christopher, ill.   II. Title.
PZ7.D3894K1   1996   [E]—dc2094-19112CIP   AC r95
ISBN 0-689-80520-9

E
DEL

DeLuise, Dom.

King Bob's new clothes

DATE DUE

3	AM-K	1	
PM-K	AM-K		
3	1	2	
PM-K	4	AM-K	
PM-K	S	2	
AM-K	2	AM-K	
AM-K	AM-K	2	
1	12	AM-K	
PM-K	14	2	
1	AM-K	PM-K	
PM-K	PM-K		
AM-K	—